D1360142

I

HATE

Reading

How to Get Through 20 Minutes of Reading Without *Really* Reading

BY **ARTHUR** & **HENRY BACON**
AS TOLD TO **BETH BACON**

Published by Pixel Titles

PO Box 4649

Rollingbay, WA

98061-0649

(781) 369-5070

ISBN 978-0-692-84282-9

Categories: 1. Juvenile nonfiction. 2. Juvenile humor.

Keywords: humor, library, boys, reading,
learning to read, reluctant readers.

I. Authors: Bacon, Arthur; Bacon, Beth; Bacon, Henry.
II. Title: I Hate Reading. Subtitle: How To Get Through 20
Minutes of Reading a Day Without Really Reading.

Design by Headquarters
(Corianton Hale & Jason Grube)
www.hqtrs.co

I ♥ HATE Reading

SCENE 1

Okay,
you have to
read for

20
MINUTES

but you don't
want to.

MAYBE YOUR MOM EVEN HAS A TIMER...

YIKES.

Here's the best book for you.

THIS
ONE

RIGHT HERE

SCENE 2

These next pages are the most important. They are a list of **RULES.**

RULE #1

Look at the book and move
your eyes from side to side.
Slowly. Eyes on book.

RULE #2

Stay in your seat.
Butt on chair.

RULE #3

Repeat rules 1 and 2 over and over
for 20 minutes or until a grown up
says you're done.

EYES ON BOOK.
BUTT ON CHAIR.

SCENE 3

Reading is not so bad when the words are EASY. Here are some easy words.

TO, I, AND.
AND, I, TO.

OK, OK, OK, OK.

NO, NO, NO.

Oh yes. A!

A is an easy word, too. It's the easiest of all. We can't forget A.

A, a, a, a, a, a, a, a, a

a, a, a, a, a, a, a, a, a.

SCENE 4

Here are some really **HARD** words. If you don't know what they say, just move your eyes from side to side.

SIDE .... TO →

SIDE ....

SIDE .... TO →

Butt on chair.

SIDE

TO · · · · · · · · · · SIDE

SIDE

Eyes on book.

Archipelago.

Plateau.

Plutonium.

Photosynthesis.

Pathatookoo.

(Tricked you, that's not a real word.)

Or, you could
just skip it.

YEAH, JUST SKIP IT. →

SCENE 5

AH-HA!

You turned the page!

(We skipped those
big words too.)

OK.

Here are some reading tips from Henry.

HENRY HATES TO READ, SO HIS TIPS WILL BE GOOD.

TIP

First, pretend you have to go to the bathroom.

Bring
the book with
you into the
bathroom. Tell
your mom you
were reading
in there.

Pick a book that has

BIG
PICTURES

and small sentences.

TIP

HUMOR

Funny books seem to go by fast.

TIP

DISTRACT

YOUR PARENTS

If they are really busy,
they will not notice you
are not reading.

SCENE 6

You are still here? **WOW**, that is pretty good. Here are tips from Arthur.

When you are in
the car, always read
the signs you see.

READ OUT LOUD. THAT WAY YOUR MOM AND DAD WILL THINK YOU READ ALL DAY LONG.

NOTE:
If you are in a car, and your parents want you to read a book, do what I do and say you get car sick. Throwing up is a good way to stop reading.

Speaking of that, bloody noses work, too. They are as good as throw-up.

SCENE 7

DEDICATED TO
EVERYONE WHO
HATES READING.

(The dedication is usually
at the beginning of a book.
Or at the end. But we forgot
and put it in the middle.)

SCENE 8

The rest of Arthur's tips:

STARE

Stare at the page. If you stare long enough, it will look like you are reading.

TIP

CHORES

Maybe your parents will let you do chores instead of reading.

WASHING THE CAR IS FUN, IF IT'S NOT TOO COLD OUTSIDE.

MATH

Do your math

homework instead

of reading.

Hey, it's something.

SCENE 9

I sometimes read.

CONFESSION FROM HENRY:

(But not often.)

SCENE 10

WHAT'S THAT RULE AGAIN?

Eyes on book,
Butt on barnacle?

Eyes on book,
Butt on toboggan?

Eyes on book,
Butt on hay bale?

Oh yeah...

EYES ON

BO

OK

BUTT ON

CHAIR.

(REPEAT FOR

20 MINUTES)

SCENE 11

Try not to get caught
NOT reading.

Here is
Henry's story:

I got caught not reading once in first grade. I was just looking at the pictures in my book

Then the teacher, Miss Gonzalez, asked, "Henry, are you just looking at the pictures?"

And I was. The pictures were real good. I looked up at Miss Gonzalez, then I turned to a page with lots of words and I put my eyeballs back on the book. She left me alone.

SCENE 12

Didn't that feel good? You got to turn the page without having to read.

I wish all books had

blank pages like that.

SCENE 13

ABOUT THE SCENES IN THIS BOOK.

What's the difference between a scene and a chapter?

Scenes are
in movies

and chapters
are in books.

WE KNOW. THIS IS NOT A MOVIE. BUT WE LIKE MOVIES BETTER.

(We bet you do, too.)

**THAT REMINDS US
OF ANOTHER TIP.**

Pretend

your book

is a movie.

SCENE 14

VACATION READING

If you are on vacation and your parents make you read, do what we do. After a long day of touring around, ask if you can lie down while you read. Ask your parents to lie down, too. You will probably all fall asleep.

SCENE 15

What to do about the kids at school who actually LIKE to read.

HUMOR

Tell them a joke. Then tell them another and another.

They will laugh
and stop reading.

SHOES

Point out that their shoes are untied.

This works for zippers too, even if their zippers are not down.

TIP

If your classroom has any **MAN-EATING ANIMALS,** put the kids who like to read in the box with them.

(Without any books.)

SCENE 16

OK, we're done.

AH

HA!

TRICKED YOU!

It's been 20 minutes. Well, maybe only 10.

But you have been reading, and you can't say you were just looking at the pictures because there aren't any.

THE

IT'S OVER

Why are you still reading?

GOOD

BYE!

THE

END

FOR REAL!

You're kidding, right?

GO PLAY!

CPSIA information can be obtained
at www.ICGtesting.com
Printed in the USA
LVIC04n2346280417
531954LV00005B/5